TROUBLE BY ANY NAME

A Western Novella

A.T. BUTLER

"I knew you'd get him, Payne," Sheriff Williams said.

When bounty hunter Jacob Payne handed over the stinking, nearly unconscious horse thief, the sheriff grabbed hold of the upper arms of the drunk before he fell on his face on the hard wooden floor. The older, heavyset man pushed and shuffled the thief back into one of the dirty cells of the Bennettsville jail before he came back out to give the bounty hunter his reward.

Jacob had turned to gaze out the window of the jail while he waited. His tall, built frame filled the entire window as he looked out, his dusty coat fitting snuggly over his broad shoulders. He watched the small town bustle. Shop owners stood in their doorways to greet passersby. Women in starched bonnets stopped to talk to their neighbors as they passed on the boardwalk. Small children pulled free of their mothers and ran out into the street, kicking up dust as they played and dodging horses. Bennettsville was a small town. Even from here Jacob could feel their affection for one another.

Jacob had learned of the reward and picked up the trail of the horse thief, Ted Glassey, outside Tucson. The trail was plain as day, as though it hadn't even occurred to Glassey that someone might try to follow him. He had only stolen a single horse, after all. Surely not worth the trouble for most bounty hunters. But Jacob Payne didn't get to be the best by turning up his nose at small rewards. Each new opportunity gave him a chance to learn, to get better, and to add more to his savings.

The thief's track had led Jacob to a dry riverbed a few miles outside Bennettsville. Glassey had built a fire. He was keeping it small, but not small enough to hide from Jacob, whose keen sense of smell was a unique advantage he had over other lawmen. It was that same unique advantage that drew him straight to the camp-fire. He tied his horse down fifty yards away and crept up to Glassey's camp on foot.

Once he got close enough, he saw he needn't have worried. Glassey was passed out drunk, whiskey bottle in hand. Without even having opened his bed roll. Jacob walked right up to the thief, pulled the bottle from his grasp, and bound his wrists without the other man even waking up.

Now that he had brought the prisoner back to town and secured the reward, Jacob could think about his next steps. His dark hair, almost black, was more shaggy than he was used to. Jacob made a mental note to visit the barber before he left town. It was easier to live rough without messy hair to fall in his face. But after that, he could be on his way. He'd find the next outlaw that needed to be taken down and make the country safer.

"He give you much trouble, Payne?" Sheriff Williams asked as he reentered the office.

Jacob shook his head. "Nope. The man was already passed out when I found him. Seemed surprise anyone came after him, to be honest. Thought he was better hidden in the brush than he really was. It was just a matter of getting him on his horse and in the direction of the jail."

"Easy money, sounds like."

"Sure. But I didn't come all the way to Arizona because it's easy."

Sheriff Williams nodded and lowered his bulk into the narrow wooden chair behind his desk. He rummaged in the bottom drawer, pulled out a sack of cash, and counted out the twenty dollars that was Jacob's due.

"You'll return the horse?" Jacob asked.

The sheriff nodded. "I'll take care of it, get word to them at the Triple S Ranch. Where will you go now? Not enough trouble in Bennettsville to tempt you, I'm guessing."

"Nope. You're doing a fine job here all on your own. I can be of more use somewhere else." Jacob examined the wall of wanted posters by the door. "What can you tell me about this'n?" He pointed to the dead-or-alive price for Elliott "Slippery" Stone. Three thousand dollars was a sizable reward.

Sheriff Williams shook his head. "Haven't heard head or tail of the Slippery Stone Gang in months. Makes me nervous. Like they may be planning something big. That one, though." He pointed to the next poster over. "Jeremiah Blanchard, with the five-hundred-dollar reward, I might have some info on. A few days ago there was a stranger come through here who claimed he saw a man fitting that description just up the road in San Adrian."

"You think that's true?"

Sheriff Williams leaned forward on the desk. "He seemed certain. The man said this was the new sheriff of San Adrian going by a different name."

"The sheriff?"

He leaned back in his chair, folding his hands over his belly. "Seems the last sheriff died and this new man up and took over a month or so ago. Stranger what came through here didn't say much else. Didn't seem to want to stay long, neither. Might be some trouble over in San Adrian even if this isn't your man."

"I'll check it out," Jacob said. He read over the poster's details. He'd be looking for a short man. Of course, most men were short compared to Jacob, but this Jeremiah character was barely over five feet. Dark hair beginning to gray. Scar along the man's left cheek. "Poster says he's wanted for murdering his wife and her parents. How'd such a despicable character make it all the way out here without getting caught?"

Sheriff Williams shook his head. "That's the way of it sometimes. It's why I became a lawman."

Jacob studied the drawing, committing the man's face to memory. "Says here he's from Virginia."

"You familiar with it?"

"Might be. Might have been there once. Feels like a long time ago, though."

"Might be useful for you."

"Might be. Did this stranger say what the new name was?"

"Horne. Sheriff John Horne. He ain't been there that long, but this ain't the first time I've heard stories come out of that town."

"All since the last sheriff died?"

Williams nodded. "Seems to be more good folk leaving there than going. If this new sheriff is a murderer, that might explain some of their unease."

Jacob raked his eyes over the other wanted posters lining the wall by the door. All the known members of the Slippery Stone Gang, of course, but also a motley collection of murderers, bank robbers, smugglers, rapists, and all manner of bad men running loose. Many people might look down on bounty hunters, call them killers or profiteers and sneer at them for taking money to kill people, but Jacob didn't see it that way. He was just one more member of law enforcement. If he took a bigger financial reward than a sheriff or U.S. Marshal, it's because he took a bigger risk as well.

As was the case now. Jacob was about to head into a dangerous situation, all on his own, with only his revolver and his wits to defend him.

"Well, it seems I have an appointment with Sheriff Horne, then," Jacob said. "Appreciate your help and the info."

"Glad to," Sheriff Williams said. "You've been a great help to me, not having a deputy. Next time you're in Bennettsville, you're welcome. I'll buy you a drink."

Jacob tipped his hat in thanks as he went out the door. He tucked his twenty dollars deep in his pocket and strode off to find the tonsorial parlor before his several-hour ride to San Adrian.

CHAPTER TWO

Jacob guided his pinto along the twelve miles to San Adrian. He kept one eye on the horizon and one eye on the brush. Snakes, scorpions, and tarantulas would usually stay away from horses out here in the desert, but Jacob followed the wisdom that you never could be too careful.

The sun was climbing in the sky. Jacob had plenty of water and turned his attention to the task ahead of him.

He needed to consider his plan of attack. In his last nine months of bounty hunting, nearly all of his targets had either fought back and shot at him once they realized they had been caught, or gave themselves up and hoped to live another day. This time could be different. This time his target had already spent weeks to get the town on his side and could lean on that new alliance to escape. Jacob would have to break that link.

As he rode into San Adrian later that morning, Jacob felt the unsettling chill of a town under pressure. There was a muted quality about it, like the weight of a heavy quilt tamping down the town's energy. Hardly anyone was out in the street, unusual for the lunch hour when he arrived and a stark contrast to Bennettsville earlier that day. The few citizens that were outside kept their heads down, watching their feet, not making eye contact with Jacob or with each other. He didn't even try to say hello.

Not very sociable, he thought to himself. No wonder people are leaving this place.

He trotted slowly up the center of the main thoroughfare in San Adrian, toward the brick hotel at the end of the street. No friendly waves or neighborly greetings found him along the way. It was as though the citizens of the town didn't want to be seen, like they were hiding from something.

Or someone.

At the end of the main street stood the Wildflower Hotel, the tallest building in town at three stories. Jacob tied up his horse outside and made his way in.

The lobby was deserted this time of day. An older woman met Jacob at the counter. A small, ludicrously feathered hat sat atop her tight gray curls. Jacob wondered if the woman's aim was to be memorable or if she just didn't realize how ridiculous the thing truly was.

"Good morning, ma'am. You have a room available tonight?"

She glanced over his shoulder toward the front door. "You may call me Mrs. Finch. I might find something for you. What business do you have in San Adrian? How long do you think you'll be here?"

Jacob shrugged. "A day or two. I've got business with the new sheriff. Horne, I think I heard his name was."

Mrs. Finch pursed her lips. She didn't comment but paused before she pulled out her ledger for Jacob to sign in.

Jacob noticed her hesitation. "Beg your pardon, Mrs. Finch, but I've never met the new sheriff. Is there anything I should know?"

She visibly relaxed after that, and she handed Jacob the pen. "Oh, well, that's all right then. We've had all kinds come through here these last few weeks, all looking for Sheriff Horne and all making trouble during the time they're here. I thought you might be one of them."

"No, ma'am. I apologize for worrying you. I was sent here by the sheriff of Bennettsville to look into a couple things. What kind of trouble you been having?"

"All kinds. Cheatin' at cards, putting wild stories in the ears of some of the boys around here, harassing poor women just trying to do their shopping. If he weren't the sheriff, I might think Mr. Horne was trying to take over this town, the way his friends seem to be scaring everyone away from San Adrian."

Jacob kept what he knew to himself. This Horne fellow wasn't a sheriff. Not really.

"Do you know he has four deputies now?" Mrs. Finch shook her head. "Four. Never before has San Adrian needed such firepower. I've not seen the like."

"Has anyone talked to him about these new strangers coming into town?"

"Well, my husband tried. Mr. Finch owns this hotel, you know. One of the most important men in town, of course." She leaned forward conspiratorially. "But he didn't want to make more trouble. When the sheriff threatened him with his pistol and told Mr. Finch to mind his own business, he dropped it. And if Sheriff Horne's new friends all stopped staying here? We'd be out of business. Besides, it's hard to tell a man he's doing wrong when he's wielding a gun and surrounded by four armed deputies."

Jacob filed this information away. He would have to come up with a way to get Sheriff Horne on his own. He didn't want to have to fight his way through a crowd of men all armed and deputized to uphold their bastardized version of the law.

"Thank you very kindly, Mrs. Finch. I'll keep all that in mind. I wonder if I could trouble you for one more thing. Can you tell me where I might get lunch around here?"

"Well, I can set you up with some biscuits and jerky to take with you, but if you'd like a hot meal then the best place is Ed's saloon up the road a bit. We used to have a proper diner, but Sally packed up and moved north after just a couple weeks of dealing with Sheriff Horne's men." She shook her head again.

"Think I passed the saloon on my way here. Ed? He the owner?"

Mrs. Finch nodded. "Ed Baker owns the place and tends the bar. His wife cooks, but they only serve food at meal times, so you'd best hurry and get over there before lunch is over. The Bakers have lived here as long as San Adrian's been standing, but things have got so bad, even Ed is talking about pulling up stakes."

Jacob thanked the hotel proprietress and said his good-byes. He led his horse to the livery and paid for food and stabling for a couple days. He didn't know how long he'd need to stick around to capture Blanchard, but the pinto could take a well-earned rest while he was in town. Next, Jacob sought out his hot lunch. Without crowds of people or gregarious shop-keepers trying to get his attention, he had no trouble finding the saloon just a few blocks east of the hotel.

When he entered, everyone in the room turned to look. At the sight of a stranger some of the customers just turned away again, but three or four took the time to glare at him, turn a cold shoulder and do whatever they could to make him feel unwelcome without making trouble. He could understand it. From their perspective, he was just one more stranger come to descend on San Adrian and wreak havoc.

"Y'all got coffee?" Jacob asked as he sat down at the bar across from its tender, a bald older man with a salt-and-pepper beard.

"Give me a few minutes and I'll make you a fresh pot."

"Thanks. You Ed? Name's Jacob Payne. Mrs. Finch sent me, said you'd be serving lunch about this time."

Ed nodded. "You almost missed it, but I'll have my wife fix you a plate. Anything else?"

"No, sir. Not right now."

Ed left to start the coffee, and Jacob turned his attention to the rest of the saloon's patrons. He was the only one sitting at the bar, but diners sat at more than half the room's tables. Jacob felt as if the other customers, mostly men, were watching him, waiting for him to give some kind of clue as to his loyalties or his business. The room was full of chatter, but Jacob couldn't make out any individual conversations.

A few minutes later, Ed came back out to the bar, hands full with a plate of roasted chicken and potatoes and a cup of coffee. It smelled delicious and Jacob heard his stomach growl. He was used to it; he often went without meals while on the road, so focused on tracking down criminals as he was.

Ed set the plate and mug down in front of Jacob, then stepped a short distance away and started wiping down dirty glasses. He glanced at

Jacob every few seconds as he did so, as though wary he might try something.

"Where can I find Sheriff Horne?" Jacob asked as he took his first bite of hot, buttery potatoes. He kept his voice down. He didn't know who any of the other customers were. One might be the outlaw's right-hand man.

"Well," Ed started slowly. "If you hadn't told me Mabel Finch had sent you, I might not be willing to say. I don't like to get on the sheriff's bad side. But as far as I know, he might be comin' here tonight for supper or cards. That's the best I can offer you. Says he has a lot of cleaning up to do after Sheriff Winthrop died. Paperwork or some such. He stays shut inside the jail most days."

"Really?" Jacob took a drink of his coffee.

Ed nodded, keeping his attention on the dusty mug under his rag. "No one's really sure what he's doing there, but your best bet if you want to go find him is to show up at the jail."

"Thanks for the tip."

Jacob took his time finishing his chicken and potatoes, all the while watching the other customers in the saloon. To a man, they all looked cowed. The chatter that filled the room wasn't the cheerful, sociable conversations he expected to hear over lunch. They were frantic, whispered discussions, hurried meals so the men and women could leave again quickly. He put down a dollar for his meal and drink and strode through the door.

Time to find the man going by the name Sheriff Horne.

CHAPTER THREE

All the shutters of the San Adrian jail were closed, blocking out the world. No light shone inside; no hint of movement. Jacob hadn't seen anyone so much as walk by this part of the street. Since he'd first arrived, the afternoon sun had sunk from high in the sky to halfway down to the horizon, softly warming his weather-worn face.

For nearly three hours the bounty hunter stood across the street and watched the building. He was used to waiting. Many times, on a tracking, he would have to sit for days waiting for a target to show themselves. This time, though, he had a full belly and a shady spot to wait. It felt almost too easy.

For the last few hours, Jacob saw no movement nor even a hint that the building was occupied. Finally, he started to consider the possibility that it wasn't. Maybe he had been waiting outside an empty building this whole time. Maybe he was wrong and this so-called sheriff was out there doing good, making an arrest or saving a child from a well.

Then Jacob reminded himself of Jeremiah Blanchard's crimes. A man who would murder a woman in cold blood wouldn't be taking his time to help any child. A man on the run all the way from Virginia wouldn't waste his time serving San Adrian's citizens. Jacob just needed to lay eyes on Sheriff Horne, confirm it was the same man going by a different name, and make his arrest.

The bounty hunter hoped it would be as easy as that. He always tried to take his targets alive when possible, but if a man pointed a gun at him it was either kill or be killed.

And Jacob wasn't aiming to be killed.

Just as he was beginning to think he had wasted his afternoon and should give up to try somewhere else, the front door of the jail opened. Three men walked out onto the wooden boardwalk.

At this distance, Jacob couldn't hear what they were saying but could read their gestures sure enough. The shortest one seemed to be the man in charge. He was bearded with long, dark hair showing streaks of gray. He didn't even bother to pull his hat down to hide his face. Jacob saw immediately that this was Jeremiah Blanchard. The other two men seemed to be listening to Blanchard give them instructions, leaning their heads in deference to him.

None of the three noticed the bounty hunter watching them from just across the street. It wasn't until a fourth and fifth man exited the building that any of the group noticed Jacob. The tallest of the men looked both ways up and down the street. Since nearly all the other citizens of the town were avoiding being seen outside, Jacob was impossible to miss, casually leaning against the wooden side of the building opposite the jail.

The tall man pointed at Jacob and yelled. "You! What do you want? Don't you have anywhere else to be?"

Jacob stepped away from the building and pushed his coat back so Jeremiah and the deputies could see his weapon. He took a few steps forward until he stood in the middle of the dusty street. The men remained on the boardwalk in front of the jail.

"Afternoon, gentlemen. I'm hoping you can help me. I'm looking for Jeremiah Blanchard."

The sheriff's expression got hard, his eyes like coal, his teeth all but bared. Now that he was close, Jacob was even more sure this was the man he sought. There was the scar trailing the left side of his face, clear as day.

One of the deputies, the oldest one wearing an all-white beard, similarly tried to stare Jacob down. He slowly drew his weapon from its holster—not yet pointing it at Jacob, but ready. That gun made Jacob think twice about capturing Jeremiah then and there. As he'd expected, Blanchard wouldn't make this easy.

The other three deputies seemed plainly confused by this stranger in the street.

"Don't know anyone by that name," one said. "What's your business with him?"

"What about you, boys? Deputy Barnes, Deputy Conroy?" the sheriff asked the older man who had drawn his gun and the tall, barrel-chested man. "Does that name sound familiar to you? You ever heard of a Jeremiah Blanchard?"

They shook their heads but kept their eyes on Jacob.

"He's wanted for murder in Virginia," the bounty hunter said, "and I got a tip he might've made it all the way out here."

"Murder?" asked the young, lanky deputy.

Jacob nodded and turned his attention to the alleged sheriff. "Murdered his wife and her elderly parents."

Deputy Conroy spit and shook his head. "What's this man look like?"

Jacob paused, acting like he had to think about it. Best not show all his cards. Not yet. "Short. Dark hair with gray in it. You have his wanted poster? It'd be a lot easier than me trying to describe him."

"What's the matter, you deaf?" Deputy Barnes asked. "Ain't we just told ya we ain't heard that name?"

"Huh," Jacob said, deliberately casual. "And you're sure you didn't see that name on any of the wanted posters in there? That seems strange. Woulda thought at least news that the bastard's wanted would get out to San Adrian, even if *he* didn't."

"Look, Mister . . . ?" Sheriff Horne began.

"Payne," Jacob supplied. He strolled closer to his target, showing the man he wasn't afraid.

"Mr. Payne. We appreciate your concern. But as you might have heard, I've only recently taken over as sheriff of this town. What my predecessor might've done with that particular wanted poster I cannot say."

"You're telling me you lost a wanted poster? What happens if someone comes in with his body? How will you identify him?"

The man shrugged. "If that happens, we can figure it out then. I tell you, it's a mess around here. Haven't even had time to look over those posters myself. But I can look for you. Jonathan Blanch, you said?"

"Jeremiah. Blanchard." Jacob spoke with exaggerated diction. "From Virginia. Y'all ever been there?"

Sheriff Horne smiled menacingly. "Can't say I have."

Can't say, or *won't say*? thought Jacob.

"Beautiful place, Virginia," Jacob said, smiling back. "Man must've done a terrible thing to get over leaving that paradise and make it all the way out here to hide in this parched country."

"Well, of course, anyone could say the same thing about you or me, Mr. Payne. Tell me, what are you doing here in the Territory of Arizona?"

Jacob shrugged. "This and that. I've my reasons for leaving back east. None of them are murder, though."

There was a heavy pause as the bounty hunter and sheriff exchanged threatening glares.

"I think you've wasted enough of our time,

Mr. Payne," Sheriff Horne said finally. He rested his hand on the butt of his gun but didn't draw it; the implication that he could was enough. He stayed on the boardwalk, which made a man of his height just tall enough to look Jacob in the eye. "I'd hate to have to run you out of town for being a menace to my citizens."

Jacob held the sheriff's gaze as he backed away. He didn't need to be told twice. He'd retreat for now so he could come up with a better plan for cornering his prey. As long as the man kept pretending to be Sheriff Horne, Jacob knew there would be another chance to take down Jeremiah Blanchard.

CHAPTER FOUR

Jacob was almost back to the hotel when someone came calling.

"Wait—mister!" Jacob heard from behind him. "Mr. Payne? Wait, I want to talk to you."

He turned to see a tall, gangly blond kid running up the street. He couldn't be any older than fifteen, but carried a Navy Revolver probably older than he was and had a shiny deputy's badge pinned securely to his front.

When Jacob saw it was the young deputy, he put his hands up, away from his holsters. "Look, I agreed to leave you fellas alone for now. You gotta do the same."

"No, you got it wrong." The kid stopped before him, breathing hard. "I was deputy to Sheriff Winthrop before he died. Name's

Timothy Brady. I'm not with those guys. That's what I want to talk to you about."

Jacob lowered his hands and looked over the kid carefully. He had a snub nose, and still a lot of the child about his face. But Jacob could also see the beginnings of worry lines forming between the youth's eyebrows, as though every day was more stressful than the last for him. As though he'd been forced into adulthood before he was ready. Brady's eyes looked worried yet hopeful. Jacob knew he should at least talk to the kid.

"Well, in that case, let's talk. Maybe we can help each other."

Inside the Wildflower Hotel, Mrs. Finch met Jacob at the desk again.

"Oh, hello, Mr. Payne. Deputy Brady, what are you doing here?"

"Is there any place around here we can talk in private?" Jacob asked.

"Take my study in the back," she said, gesturing them to a small room off the lobby. "Timothy, you know where the cookies are if you boys decide you need some."

Timothy blushed a deep red. "Back here," he mumbled as he led Jacob to the room and closed the door behind them.

Jacob looked around at one of the most

opulent rooms he'd encountered since arriving in Arizona. Floral wallpaper, a full bookcase, two finely upholstered wingback chairs, and even a marble mantle above the hearth that must have cost a fortune to be shipped all the way out west. No wonder the Finches were treading lightly. Having to leave San Adrian would be disastrous for them.

"How long have you been a deputy?" Jacob began as they settled into the chairs in Mrs. Finch's study. He closed his eyes for a moment to better feel the comfort and luxury all around him. Since he spent most of his days tracking in the untamed wilderness, just a cushion under him when he sat made a world of difference.

"I started about a year ago. A lot of the town don't take me seriously yet. You heard Mrs. Finch offer us cookies." He ducked his head, as though embarrassed. "Right after I turned fourteen, my uncle Alex—he was sheriff, before Horne, see—he deputized me. I was his only one. We don't get much trouble around here. Or when we do, a U.S. Marshal comes. But I moved out here from Philadelphia with my aunt and uncle when I was just a kid, and he kept saying how much he was looking forward to working with me when I was old enough."

"What happened?"

"He died. 'Bout a month ago. The new Sheriff Horne had recently moved to town and was trying to make friends. Or so he said. He and Uncle Alex went out hunting one day and I guess just had some bad luck. Uncle Alex got bit by a rattler, and they were too far from Doctor Pike to save him in time."

"That's a shame, Deputy. I'm real sorry to hear that."

"You can call me Timothy. Everyone else does. I'm mostly sorry for my aunt Maggie. She didn't want to come west and leave her family back in Pennsylvania, but she loved Uncle Alex. And now she's widowed, with no one to take care of her but me."

"I'm sure you do a great job."

He shrugged and blushed again. "I think so. I don't know what we'd do without my deputy pay, though. I'm not a ranch hand or miner or nothin'."

"I don't think you need to worry about that. But, tell me, why did you want to talk to me?"

"I thought maybe the description you gave of that outlaw sounded familiar, but I couldn't remember. Maybe if you gave me more detail it could jog my memory."

Jacob smiled and leaned back in his chair.

"You're a good man, Deputy Brady. Timothy. The man we're looking for is short. Dark and graying hair, like I mentioned. Dark eyes. And a deeply scarred face that he tries to hide under a beard."

Timothy paled, his eyes widening like saucers. "What kind of scar?"

Jacob had hoped the boy could make the connection on his own. "It looks like a small knife—or maybe a woman's fingernail—scratched him from his left eyebrow all the way down to his jaw."

"No," Timothy whispered.

"You think you might have an idea?"

"What did you say this fella did?"

"He killed his wife. Strangled her. Then, when her parents came visiting to see where she was, he killed them, too, and left his hometown to come hide in the wide open deserts of Arizona."

"Geez," the boy said, leaning back in his chair.

"You think you know this man, Timothy?"

The boy nodded. "It's Sheriff, ain't it?"

Jacob nodded grimly. "Has to be. No matter what name he calls himself, Sheriff Horne matches the description too perfectly to be anyone else. And he's only heaping on the suspicion by mysteriously losing the wanted poster for Jeremiah Blanchard."

Timothy sat straight. "We have to do something."

Jacob hid a smile at the boy's enthusiasm. "We will. I have some ideas. But I don't know how this town will take it, seein' as how they've got a man like that in charge."

"You should talk to my aunt," Timothy said excitedly, almost bouncing in his chair now. "We've lived here for almost ten years. She knows San Adrian better than anyone. Come home to dinner with me."

"Aunt Maggie?" Timothy called as they walked in.

The Winthrops' home was a couple blocks off the main street of San Adrian, a modest, wooden house with just two rooms. The main, front room Jacob found himself in housed the kitchen and table, along with a couple chairs by the wide stone fireplace. A thin bedroll was tucked against the wall by the hearth—probably where Timothy slept.

Out of the bedroom tacked on to the back of the main room came Aunt Maggie, and Jacob was stunned for a moment. This woman didn't look old enough to be Timothy's aunt. She was lovely; she had clear white skin with just a smattering of freckles on her nose, and red-blond hair that shone in the firelight. At the top of her high neckline, she wore a delicate brooch with what looked like a lock of hair.

"Evening, ma'am," Jacob said, removing his hat.

"Aunt Maggie, this is Jacob Payne," Timothy said excitedly. "He's going to help us get Sheriff Horne out of San Adrian."

CHAPTER FIVE

After Timothy told his aunt a bit more about the stranger he had just let into their home, Maggie invited Jacob to stay for dinner. They would need to talk over what they could do to handle the new sheriff without putting themselves or anyone else in the town in danger, and Jacob was grateful for their help and insight. Intelligent conversation and two hot meals in one day? He was beginning to feel spoiled. He wanted to be sure to show her how grateful he was for her hospitality.

When Timothy went out to chop wood and gather more water, Jacob offered his assistance to Maggie.

"Is there anything round here that needs doing? Something your husband would have fixed or built, or a chore that's been waiting for the last month?"

Her eyes filled with tears.

"I'm sorry, ma'am. I didn't mean to—"

"No, no. It's fine. You're right. I'm sure there are some chores that I've been neglecting. But for now . . ."

She thought for a moment then smiled coyly and, to his surprise, actually laughed.

"What?" asked Jacob, bewildered.

"Well . . . there *is* one thing my husband used to do for me that I could use help with. But"—and here she laughed again, blushing furiously—"you won't like it."

"Whatever you need, Mrs. Winthrop. Just tell me. I aim to make myself useful as long as I'm here."

"Well." She took a deep breath as though steeling herself for something unpleasant. She ducked her chin, looking up at him through long eyelashes. "He used to peel the potatoes."

Jacob had expected something a lot worse. He grinned and nodded. "I can do that. I might not look it, but I have actually peeled potatoes before."

"Would you like an apron?" she offered, teasing him.

He was tempted to accept, just to see if he

could make her laugh again, but decided not to. She had only been a widow for a month, and it wouldn't be proper for him to be monopolizing her attention that way.

"No, ma'am. I think I can handle a few potato peels. Can't do me any more harm than riding all morning has."

She laughed again and said, "Thank you for that. I haven't laughed since my husband died."

Jacob grew serious. "I was real sorry to hear about that, Mrs. Winthrop. From what Timothy tells me, it sounds like he was a good, generous man. You should have had a long life together."

Tears welled up in the widow's eyes, but she smiled and dabbed them away before they could fall. "He was . . . he was just that. And he would hate what has become of San Adrian now."

"Don't you worry. We'll fix it. Now, where are those potatoes you need peeled?"

A short time later, after Jacob had peeled all the potatoes, Timothy had finished his chores, and Maggie had finished making dinner, the three sat down to the table together.

"I'll say grace, Aunt Maggie," Timothy volunteered.

Jacob bowed his head with the others. As the boy prayed, Jacob appreciated how both

Maggie and Timothy could be grateful for what they had and not bitter about what they had lost. It made him all the more determined to help make it right and put Jeremiah behind bars.

As the three dug into the stew Maggie had made, she commented slyly, "My, what wonderfully peeled potatoes we have here."

Jacob grinned. "My own secret recipe."

"I'm sure. Your mama teach you that? Or your wife?" She looked down into her bowl with this last question.

"I did have a wife, ma'am. But she died in the war. Truth be told, that's also where I learned to peel potatoes."

"Well, then." She smiled at him. "I guess I'll have to thank your sergeant."

Jacob couldn't help but voice a nagging thought he had been having since he'd arrived.

"Pardon me for saying so, Mrs. Winthrop, but I don't see how you're old enough to be this boy's aunt."

Maggie smiled and fixed Jacob with a humorous look. "Well, Mr. Payne, you know a lady never reveals her age."

"Of course— I . . . I'm sorry—" he stammered.

She laughed and quickly reassured him.

"Timothy's mother was my sister—my *much older* sister. When she and my brother-in-law died, there was no one else to take him in. Alex and I were not yet engaged, but he could see how badly I wanted to give this boy a home. So we got married right away and adopted the child."

"And now he's lost another parent."

Timothy was eating silently, looking down at his plate. Jacob couldn't imagine how hard this last month had been for the boy. Jacob's own relationship with his father had been strained, but at least he had been around through all of Jacob's childhood.

"How has the last month been for you?" Jacob asked Maggie.

Maggie took a bite of her stew before answering, chewing slowly and considering what to say. Jacob stayed quiet, giving her the time she needed to think about it.

"It's been hard, as you can imagine," she said. "Not just the death, but the everyday as well. We never got my husband's last month's pay." She looked down at her bowl, avoiding Jacob's eyes. "Sheriff Horne confiscated it. Claimed it was evidence."

"Evidence? Of what? What is he investigating?"

She shook her head. "I don't know. He says my Alex died of a snakebite, so I haven't a clue what the pay has to do with that."

"Did the undertaker say it was a snakebite?"

She shook her head. "No. That is, I'm not sure. We never discussed it. I just took Sheriff Horne at his word." She studied Jacob's expression. "You think I should have questioned it?"

"Maybe. Maybe not at that moment, but it might be worth looking into now. If he has your husband's pay to dole out, he might be having an easier time bringing those deputies around to his side. But, on the other hand, if we can find evidence of another murder, it might be possible to get the other deputies out of Sheriff Horne's pocket. The fewer men I have to fight to bring him to justice, the better."

Timothy paled at that. "You think you'll have to fight the other deputies?"

Jacob chewed thoughtfully. "I might. But then, there might be a way I don't have to. If the man would just admit what he and I both know, this could be a lot more simple."

He paused when he saw Maggie reach over to squeeze Timothy's hand. The boy was nervous, that was plain. But whether it was at the thought of fighting the other deputies, of his first real job as a law enforcer, or of something else, Jacob didn't know.

"I'm sorry. We don't have to talk about this at dinner."

At this, Timothy finally looked up. "No. I want to. I want to get this guy out of here, if . . . if he really did murder all those people."

Jacob nodded somberly. "He did."

"Then let's do this."

"We will. But we have to be smart about this. We don't want to start a shootout or put any of the other folks here in danger. A man who feels cornered may lash out, and we already know Jeremiah is capable of murder."

Maggie ventured, "You think we need a way to disarm Sheriff Horne—I mean, Jeremiah Blanchard?"

"Maybe. But more than that, men like him need to feel like they're in power. We need to strip him of whatever power he thinks he has."

"How do we do that?" Timothy asked.

"Leave that to me," Jacob said. "What I need from you is something different."

CHAPTER SIX

After helping Maggie wash the dishes and clean up after supper, Jacob left the little family alone for the evening. Both Timothy and Maggie had a part in the plan Jacob had come up with for the next day. He wanted to give them time, not only to rest but also to think about if the task ahead was too big of a risk. He had told them over and over that he could take the man on his own—Jacob was used to confronting dangerous men, and Maggie and Timothy were not, in spite of their connection to the previous sheriff —but they'd insisted on helping.

As he strolled along the boardwalk to the right of the street, back through the dark, quiet town, Jacob pondered what he had learned since arriving in town earlier that day.

Talking to Maggie and Timothy had shown him that not only was Sheriff Horne indeed the man he was after, but it was possible he might have another murder on his conscience as well. It seemed like too much of a coincidence that the previous sheriff died not long after the new man showed up in town.

This was a different kind of bounty than Jacob was used to. Instead of being on the run from the law, the murderer had become the law. Not only would Jacob need to overpower the man somehow, but he would also need to make sure that the rest of San Adrian was on board. Every man, woman, and child in town was upholding the criminal's authority at present. He couldn't afford to capture Sheriff Horne only to be captured himself by the gang of deputies.

After a few blocks, Jacob stopped. He looked around. The town seemed all but deserted. He looked up at the night sky; there seemed to be far more stars out here in Arizona than he remembered from his home back east. Or maybe he had just never taken the time to notice.

Lights shone out of the saloon and hotel windows, but almost no sound made it to the abandoned street where Jacob walked. Most of the homes around the Winthrops' were dark and shuttered.

This, more than anything, told him things were off in San Adrian. The one night he spent in Bennettsville, for example, Jacob was greeted with music, laughter, and friendly hey-theres when he walked through town at this same time of night. Here it was different. The people were hiding.

Just before he reached the main street, only a few blocks away from the Winthrops', Jacob heard steps behind him. He paused, looked back, but didn't see anyone. He decided to move from walking along the boardwalk in front of the buildings to walking in the middle of the dusty street. There would be fewer shadows and fewer corners to hide an attacker.

He continued his stroll, and again he heard footsteps mingled with his own. It wasn't someone running up to meet him, but rather a stalker marking his steps, keeping in time but staying back. Jacob turned to look at who was following him, but saw only shadow against the darkened buildings. Whoever it was didn't want to be seen.

"You know I'm armed," he called into the darkness.

Silence.

"If you have something to say, then say it, 'stead of hiding in the shadows like a thief."

Silence . . . and then, from the darkness, a figure began to emerge.

The silhouette of a tall man wearing a long duster and Stetson. Jacob held his ground while the figure approached. As the mystery man closed the distance, stepping into the light spilling from the nearby hotel, the bright reflection of the man's white beard identified him as Deputy Barnes.

Jacob wondered if the sheriff had sent him to follow, or if the man was acting on his own.

He stopped twenty feet away from Jacob.

"Is there something I can help you with, sir?" Jacob asked in a biting tone. "There must be a reason you're skulking around following me."

"We don't want your kind around here."

"My *kind?*" He laughed. "What, men from Virginia? Best tell the sheriff that, then."

"A bounty hunter's got no place here. If you know what's good for you, you'll leave town. Tonight."

Jacob chuckled. "That's your big scary threat? That I should leave town? Let me tell you, mister. I don't aim to leave without Jeremiah Blanchard in tow. Dead or alive. I wasn't the first to hear about him being seen in San Adrian, and I won't be the last."

"So I should end you right now, then?" the deputy said.

Jacob shrugged. If this man meant to kill him, he'd have been shot in the back before even hearing steps behind him. The deputy may be a bad seed, but he wasn't in the same league as Jeremiah.

"I'm warning you . . ." Barnes said.

Jacob didn't move. He didn't draw his own gun, but he also didn't surrender. He wanted this man to know he could not be intimidated. They were standing in the center of the dark main street of San Adrian. It was only nine o'clock, but there was no one else around, no one to witness this bullying.

"Look, mister. There's something that's been bugging me. I don't know why you've thrown your hat in with this murderer, but if you're not careful you'll end up on a wanted poster yourself. So tell me. What's in it for you?"

Deputy Barnes looked taken aback. "What's in it for me? Other than this deputy badge that gives me leave to do whatever I want?" He laughed a hard, brusque bark.

"Surely not whatever you want," Jacob

responded. "You the type of man who'd murder a woman? Like Jeremiah?"

Still with his gun trained on Jacob, he stalked forward a couple steps. "You don't know what you're talking about."

Jacob stood his ground. "You're fooling yourself, friend. It takes a specific kind of man to murder, and not one you can count on being on your side for long. Jeremiah will use you for what he can and then discard you."

"That's all *you* know."

"Then tell me. Why should I walk away now and leave this town to his mercy?"

"Sheriff Horne is a man who gets things done," Barnes said. "Your showing up in town may have interrupted his plans temporarily, but it just bumped you to the top of his list."

Jacob shook his head, disappointed in the man's answer.

"I'll remember your face, you know," Jacob said. "As long as I'm a bounty hunter, I'll be on the lookout for those blue eyes staring out at me from a wanted bill. Doesn't even matter what name you might be going by, Deputy *Barnes*."

The deputy raised his arm, pointing his gun at Jacob's face. Jacob did not flinch. After a moment, the deputy lowered his arm, quickly firing into the dirt right at Jacob's feet.

"I won't tell you again," the deputy said with an angry growl. "The next time I see you, it had better be the back of you on a horse riding west. If you stay in San Adrian, you'll die. Just like your friend Sheriff Winthrop."

Jacob shook his head and turned his back on the deputy, to finish his walk back to his hotel room. He whistled "Battle Hymn of the Republic" as though he hadn't a care in the world.

CHAPTER SEVEN

The next morning, Jacob woke early, spent some time cleaning his gun, and made his way down to the hotel lobby. He had a few loose ends to tie up in San Adrian today, the first being to ask a favor from Mrs. Finch.

"Good morning, Mr. Payne," she said, greeting him with a smile. He eyed today's hat —a narrow gray thing, with a small veil and purple- and green-dyed feathers sticking almost straight up. "Will you be checking out today?"

"Not just yet, Mrs. Finch. I think my business will wrap up later today, but I'll hold on to the room, just in case."

"All right. Well, then, since you'll be our guest a little bit longer, can I offer you some coffee?"

"Coffee would be great. But there's also one other thing you can do for me, ma'am."

"I'm happy to help if I can."

"It's a small thing, I hope—I don't want to interrupt your day. Do you think you could see your way to coming down to the livery this afternoon? Or, probably better, the *street* in front of the livery? Say around one o'clock?"

Mrs. Finch looked confused as she poured the coffee for him. "You need me at the livery? I don't understand . . . I thought your business was with Sheriff Horne. The livery is at the opposite end of town from the jail."

"I don't want to say too much," Jacob said. "It's better if you don't know what to expect. You'll see why when you get there."

She nodded hesitantly, still puzzled. "If we don't have any guests checking in at that time, I'll be there."

"Thank you, ma'am. And thank you for the coffee. Can I get breakfast at Ed's saloon, too?"

She shook her head. "No. Sometimes Mrs. Baker has bread left over from the night before, but you won't get much more than that till lunch, I'm afraid. My offer to supply you with jerky and biscuits still stands, though."

"Thank you. I'd like that."

When Mrs. Finch left to go prepare Jacob's

lunch, he wandered out to the boardwalk in front of the hotel. There were still almost no people out in the street. He needed to do something about that. He stepped back inside.

"Mrs. Finch," he said as she returned. "If you happen to talk to any of your neighbors this morning, could you invite them to the livery as well?"

She frowned, and a hint of fear tugged at her face. "I . . . I don't understand, Mr. Payne. Are you trying to draw a crowd? Is something exciting going to happen?" The way she said the word *exciting* made him believe she meant it as anything but.

"Hopefully," he replied. "You'll see when you get there."

When he left the hotel, Jacob spotted Maggie Winthrop coming out of the telegraph office about a block over on the other side of the street. As she stepped off the wooden walkway, the train of her black dress caught on a loose corner and she stopped, bent down, and freed herself. As she stood back up, Maggie caught his eye, adjusted her bonnet, and smiled shyly, but didn't stop to talk. That was okay with Jacob. After their long conversation last night, he knew she had a full day ahead of her.

He began walking in the other direction,

toward the next item on his list to make this plan work, but was stopped in his tracks when he overheard a fight.

"I told you—that was your last chance!" a familiar voice shouted behind him. He turned slowly, moving his hand to unhook his hammer loop.

But Sheriff Horne wasn't shouting at him. The little man was sitting on his horse, glaring down at another man standing before him. It took a second, but Jacob realized this was Ed Baker, and as he watched, the sheriff reached down to slap the older man across the face.

Jacob started walking to the saloonkeeper's side, but before he could reach him, Ed was quickly surrounded by three of the sheriff's deputies. Soon Jacob had lost a clear line of sight to him.

Sheriff Horne stayed on his horse. Jacob realized that was the only way he would even be tall enough to reach Ed. "You think you're above the law, Baker? You think you know better? Better than *me*?"

Jacob reached the cluster in the middle of the street and noticed a crowd gathering to watch. Many of the women held hands over their mouths, shocked at the abuse they were witnessing, their men standing with their arms around them protectively but not doing anything to stop the abuse. Ed was beloved in this town, that much Jacob had gathered; but no one, it seemed, was brave enough to step forward to defend him.

Jacob wouldn't be so cowed.

He pushed one of the deputies out of his way just in time to stop the sheriff from hitting Ed again. "Why don't you get down off that horse if you really want a fight?"

The deputies all pushed and grabbed at Jacob, pulling him away from their boss. It took all three of them to subdue him. Jacob didn't want a fight, so he quit struggling. The deputies didn't let go.

"Stop this! What are you hitting him for?" Jacob demanded.

Jeremiah smiled condescendingly down from his perch atop the stallion. "This is San Adrian business, Mr. Payne. Seeing as you're a stranger to this town, I don't really see any reason to enlighten you."

"Ed," Jacob said in a low voice. "What happened?"

The man's cheek was still bright red where he had been smacked, and he glared at the sheriff. His eyes met Jacob's. He was angry, livid even, but still unwilling to say anything. Jacob could understand that. With his whole livelihood dependent on the goodwill of the town, it wouldn't be in his interest to make this fight worse.

"Sheriff Horne!" a woman's voice called over the crowd.

Jacob turned to see a squat redheaded woman coming from up the street and making her way between the men and women watching the scene.

"Sheriff Horne?" As she jogged toward the crowd, she untied and removed her apron, wrapping her hands in the calico. "What has Ed done? Something upset you, sir? That doesn't sound like my Ed." She reached her husband's side and put her arm around his shoulders. Mrs. Baker was a full head shorter than her husband, but she still managed to look like a protective mother hen. She used the apron in her hand to clean the dirt off Ed's hands and face from where he fell in the street.

"Well, ma'am," the sheriff said plaintively, "your husband has some outlandish ideas. Seems he thinks that *he's* the one gets to decide how things are 'round here. But maybe you're right—maybe it's not like him. Might be he picked up some things when talking to some of the more unsavory characters 'round here."

He looked pointedly at Jacob. Mrs. Baker followed his gaze and hardened her expression against the bounty hunter.

"You might be right, Sheriff Horne," she said. "We'll be sure to be more careful about who we serve from now on."

Without saying good-bye or asking the sheriff's leave, Ed and his wife cut through the crowd and back toward their saloon. Jacob was still being restrained by two of the deputies, but when he tried to shake them loose, they relaxed their grip.

"Beating an unarmed man, Sheriff? Is that the way to win hearts and minds around here?"

Jacob spat at the foot of the horse Jeremiah sat on and turned to go. As he passed, he noticed a look of concern cross Deputy Conroy's face. Jacob noted how the big man stepped back from the sheriff and thought maybe he was already making inroads.

CHAPTER EIGHT

As Jacob walked away from Sheriff Horne and his deputies in the middle of the street, he had to weave his way through the crowd that had gathered to watch the commotion. Many of the people he passed looked at him curiously, some not so friendly. Some of them were beginning to murmur to one another, and he caught snatches of conversation as he moved through the group.

"He shouldn't—"

"What could have—"

"I don't like this."

It was starting.

Jacob hoped that once the townspeople began to realize they could fight back against Sheriff Horne's dictatorship, the tide would turn. If even Deputy Conroy was beginning to change his opinion, like Jacob suspected, this might all work out without any more blood-shed. As long as the sheriff had the town's tacit support, the man could do whatever he wanted; but it looked as if that was beginning to change.

The scene Jacob was now leaving could have been the perfect opportunity to take down the sheriff—but it was too fast. Too soon. He hadn't had the proper time to collect all the pieces he needed. He'd just have to try again.

The day was beginning to warm as he walked away from the crowd, reading the signs above each storefront. He pulled out the biscuits and jerky Mrs. Finch had given him and gnawed while he looked. Jacob had one last piece of the puzzle to fit in before making a new attempt to subdue and capture the outlaw. He had a nagging suspicion, and only one person could help alleviate it.

He found the undertaker's office a block away from the jail. The sign above the door read Charles & Son Undertakers, and when Jacob walked in he found the older Mr. Charles working bent over his desk.

"Pardon me. I'm sorry to bother you, sir," Jacob said, taking his hat in hand.

"Nonsense. Come in, come in," the older

man said, standing to greet Jacob. He was slightly hunched over, as though the weight of all the deaths he had overseen remained on his shoulders. His white mustache was neatly trimmed and his spectacles clean and clear. "I'm Eugene Charles. What can I do for you, young man? Can I offer you coffee?" He looked toward the doorway behind Jacob. "You don't seem to have a body in tow."

"No, sir. Not yet, at least."

"Not yet?" Mr. Charles frowned. "Death is nothing to be flippant about, young man. But I'm forgetting myself—I don't believe we've met. You're new to San Adrian, are you not?"

"I am, Mr. Charles. Just here for a couple days, God willing. And I'm sorry—I don't mean to be flippant. I was wondering if I could ask you something."

He narrowed his eyes suspiciously. "What did you say your name was?"

"Payne. Jacob Payne." He sat in the wooden chair across the desk from Eugene and placed his hat on his knee.

"Ah, yes," the older man said, relaxing back into his chair. "I've heard of you."

This surprised Jacob. "You have?"

"Oh, yes. Ed Baker is one of my good friends, and we talked just last night. He told me you were looking for Sheriff Horne, so I thought it'd only be a matter of time before you ended up in my office."

"Oh?"

"Glad to see you're here alive, if I could speak honestly. I thought it might be possible you'd get here on a slab instead, the way you're going after the sheriff."

"Well, to be honest, sir, I still might. Again, not to be flippant about death. But Sheriff Horne is a dangerous character, and I seem to be making him mad."

He chuckled. "I bet you are."

"In fact, if I might be so bold, sir . . . you might think about looking in on your friend Mr. Baker later today. I just witnessed him being beaten and upbraided in the middle of the street by Sheriff Horne himself."

Mr. Charles frowned. "Right in the street, you say? Well. That's no way to treat a grown man, let alone a prominent citizen of the town the sheriff has sworn to protect. I'll talk to Ed about it. You said you wanted to ask me something?"

"Yes, sir. I was wondering if I could trouble you about something that's been bothering me. I understand you might not want to get involved, so I can do my best to leave your name out of it."

Eugene smiled grimly. "Just be out with it, young man."

"Well, Deputy Brady and Mrs. Winthrop told me about how Sheriff Winthrop died. I was wondering if you had seen the body, and if you could confirm it was a snakebite that killed him."

Eugene looked at Jacob, rubbing his chin thoughtfully. "What makes you ask that?"

"Just a hunch. Seems like quite a coincidence if it happened the way Horne is telling it. I would think a man like Winthrop, a man who's lived out here in the desert for years, would have more caution and know how to avoid the snakes."

Eugene nodded. "That's true. Well, Mr. Payne, I can tell you this much."

Jacob sat forward, leaning on his elbows.

"Sheriff Winthrop did indeed suffer a snakebite. Based on my examination, it did seem to be from a rattler, but I can't be completely positive."

"All right, then. Thank you—"

"But that's not all."

Jacob abruptly shut his mouth to listen.

"The snakebite appeared to have happened after the man was already dead."

"What?" It felt as if a stone had dropped into the pit of Jacob's stomach. This was as bad as he suspected. "How can you be sure?"

"There was no blood around the bite wound. The poor man had likely already bled out from a bullet to the gut."

"A bullet to the gut? That's a lot of blood . . . how is it no one else saw the gut wound?"

"Hard to say, but I would guess that Horne—excuse me, *Sheriff* Horne—put Sheriff Winthrop's vest and jacket back on the corpse after the wound occurred."

"That's despicable."

Mr. Charles nodded. "How he managed that, I can't say. We can't be sure about the sequence of events unless Sheriff Horne tells us himself. Putting the clothes back on after the fact would have hid the blood from anyone giving the body a cursory look and would not have been discovered until my son took over management of the corpse."

Jacob leaned back in his chair, shaking his head. Just hearing about a man using the law as a cover to get away with murder made him incredibly angry. Angry as a man who was loyal to the law. Angry on behalf of Maggie and

Timothy and what they had lost. Angry on behalf of all the citizens of San Adrian, like Ed Baker.

"Did you tell anyone else what you found?"

Eugene shook his head. "My son knows, of course, but he's discreet. Who would I tell? The new sheriff or one of his thugs? No, I kept that information to myself. Winthrop was already dead, and I thought it best to not make waves with the new man in charge."

"If I am able to capture Sheriff Winthrop and bring him to justice, would you be willing to testify against him?"

"If he's captured? If he's brought to trial, then yes. I will tell all that I know. But as long as he is running this town, I trust you'll keep this information to yourself."

"Why tell me, if I may ask? You're not worried about me revealing it?"

"The way I see it, Mr. Payne, if you're going after this man, you are at even bigger risk than I am. It can't possibly do you any good to reveal this information unless you're absolutely sure it will be to your success."

Jacob nodded and stood to say good-bye. "Very true, Mr. Charles. I take it you've worked with a lot of lawmen in your life."

The older man smiled. "They come and go,

and yet I'm still here. Good luck to you, young man."

With that confirmed, Jacob knew it was time. He had all the pieces he needed lined up to kill or capture Jeremiah Blanchard.

CHAPTER NINE

When he left the undertaker's, it was almost one o'clock. The morning had gone by quickly, but he had to trust that enough time had passed for what Jacob was planning. He had an appointment—the last domino that needed to fall before he could capture Jeremiah without difficulty from the rest of the town. It would be a risk, but it was the only way Jacob knew to get close to the sheriff; otherwise, there would always be a deputy in the way.

The undertaker's office was near the jail, but Jacob walked right past it without even a glance. He was looking for another target—the stretch of main street out front of the livery. It would be almost as far away as he could get from the jail and still be in San Adrian.

As he approached, he counted four or five people standing outside the door, including Sheriff Horne's loyal deputies. Jacob scanned the crowd quickly, grateful that Maggie wasn't there to see what was about to happen. She knew about this step; perhaps she was avoiding the scene on purpose. That was just fine, Jacob thought.

As Jacob closed the final yards before the crowd, he steeled himself. What he was about to do would not be pleasant, but it would be necessary. A common trait of the job.

"You," he bellowed. "You think you can spread stories about me and I won't find out?"

The waiting crowd all turned to see who was yelling. Most of them backed up when they saw Jacob bearing down on them with all his six-plus feet of muscle. Only Deputy Brady held his ground, defiantly raising his chin and answering in the affirmative—just as they'd practiced.

"You're the one telling tales on me?"

"That's right, Payne. I— I did," Timothy said as he stood up straighter and squared his shoulders. "What are you going to do about it?"

He must have dug deep for his bravado. Anyone could see Jacob was at least twice his body weight, nearly all of it in muscle. The bounty hunter loomed over the kid. He kept his hands off his gun but took his coat off and threw it in the dust to give himself greater range of movement. He rolled his sleeves up as Timothy backed up a couple steps.

Jacob shoved Timothy off the boardwalk and into the dusty street. The kid stumbled, backing up several long steps into the road. A man riding past had to swerve his horse out of the way, and shouted at Timothy as he did.

Jacob jumped down off of the wooden planks to go after Timothy, the dust creating clouds around his feet. "Deputy Brady," he said. "Only a coward would run now."

His voice was cold, but he tried to communicate something different to Timothy with his eyes. Jacob realized they should have discussed this part of the plan in a little more detail before now.

"Hey!" one of the deputies yelled.

Jacob shot him a look of loathing, wordlessly daring him to interrupt. He did not.

Timothy recovered his balance. "Stay out of this, Deputy Conroy, Deputy Nelson," he called to the crowd still standing around the livery. "This is between me and Payne."

Jacob had reached the kid and used both his wide palms to shove him in the chest, knocking him to the ground. Timothy landed hard on his rear, accidentally putting his hand in a stinking pile of manure that had been dropped not long ago. The look of disgust on the deputy's face came and went in a flash. He didn't dwell. He shook it off and wiped his hand on his pants.

Jacob wrinkled his nose reflectively. That smell . . . he'd need to be even more diligent about not letting the kid hit him.

Timothy scrambled to his feet and held up his fists in front of him, as though he had the slightest idea how to fight. He bounced on the balls of his feet, ready to dart to the right or left depending on how Jacob came at him.

"Goodness, someone stop them!" a woman cried.

Jacob didn't bother to see who. The more people that gathered, the better. The more citizens the woman called to the scene to witness what should be about to happen, the more smoothly Jacob's plan would work.

The look of fear on Timothy's face almost made Jacob hesitate, but he knew better. This was what had to happen. Timothy was as good as a grown man now, and a deputy of the law would know he was at risk for this. This was what he wanted, too; Jacob had given him plenty of opportunity to back out.

Jacob reeled back and swung, punching

Timothy in the jaw and knocking him to the dirt.

"Oh my!" Mrs. Finch exclaimed.

Timothy climbed to his feet and rushed Jacob, putting his shoulder down and running hard at him. When the kid made contact, Jacob had to back up a few steps but managed to hold his ground. He wrapped his arms around the kid and tossed him a few feet away from him.

"You think you can just throw me around?" Timothy cried at him as he regained his balance, his voice cracking. "I'm a deputy! You can't put your hands on me. Wait till I tell Sheriff Horne."

Jacob punched Timothy in the nose, wincing at the crack he both felt and heard. Timothy stumbled backward a few paces before losing his footing and landing in the dirt yet again. Blood bloomed from the boy's nostrils, dripping down over his mouth. He spat a bloody mist to the ground near Jacob's feet. The boy had yet to knock the bounty hunter down, and Jacob almost felt bad.

"You do that. You call Sheriff Horne. That's exactly the man I want to see. He should be here protecting his deputy, but where is he? The coward."

Timothy's eyes grew wide at Jacob's declaration. "I don't— I think maybe—"

"Call him," Jacob continued, turning to the crowd to address them as well. "We already know Horne isn't man enough to keep control of this town without resorting to violence. We all saw him attacking an unarmed man earlier."

"Jacob," Timothy said softly.

"Stop right there," a voice said behind the bounty hunter.

But Jacob didn't stop. He pulled Timothy to his feet, only so he could punch him to the ground again.

"Stop, I say. You are assaulting an officer of the law!" The voice was closer now, but still Jacob didn't stop.

A crack rang out, crashing through Jacob's focus and interrupting his attack. After half a second, he realized his left arm hurt. No, it *burned*. And when he paused in his punching to reach up and touch the spot, his fingers came away wet and red.

He had been shot.

His plan may be unraveling.

CHAPTER TEN

Jacob was still looking at the blood on his fingers when he heard, "Jacob Payne, you are under arrest for assaulting an officer."

Deputy Timothy Brady lay in the dirt at Jacob's feet, wincing as he felt his jaw and checked to make sure all his teeth were still in his head. His nose had bled a bit, staining the front of his shirt, and was quickly swelling up. Jacob hoped he hadn't hurt him too bad. The kid had a manic gleam of triumph in his eyes—even through the injury, he was enjoying himself.

The gunfire had paused the fight. In the lull, the other three deputies rushed to seize Jacob and stop him from attacking Timothy further. Two grabbed each of his massive arms, while the third stabbed him in the back with the barrel of his revolver.

A crowd was fully gathered now. Jacob noticed Mrs. Finch's hat standing tall like the mast of a ship above the heads of the others, the green and purple feathers glinting in the sun. She had come just as he'd asked her to. He hoped she would be quick enough to understand why. Their shouting and carrying on had drawn many of the other citizens of San Adrian to the crowd as well.

But, as he looked around at the crowd surrounding them, he cringed. Jacob had not intended to get shot. His carefully crafted plan was showing cracks. The whole left side of his body felt heavy as the blood drained from his arm. He made a brief attempt to shake the deputies off, but he didn't have the strength to fight back against three grown men holding him immobilized.

None of the crowd came to defend him. And why would they? They hadn't done anything earlier, when the sheriff was beating Ed Baker for no good reason. Why would they lift a finger in protest now, when this stranger had clearly provoked his own attack?

"You have no authority to arrest me," Jacob said through clenched teeth.

From behind him Deputy Nelson said, "You shut up, Payne. You were caught attacking a deputy. You can't get away with that."

"Where's Blanchard?"

"Who?"

"Your boss. He told you he's Sheriff Horne, but he's a murderer by any name. Jeremiah Blanchard."

"You shut up," Deputy Conroy said, punching Jacob in the mouth.

Shot, restrained, and now punched, Jacob was feeling his prey slip through his fingers. "Where is he?" he yelled.

The deputy punched him again, and Jacob felt his teeth smash against his lower lip. He spat out a mouthful of blood at the feet of his assaulter.

"Bring him here."

Jacob tried to glance behind him, where Jeremiah Blanchard stood in the middle of the street, forcing the few riders to either go around him or stop altogether. Jacob had wanted a crowd, and now his target was helping him create one.

Jeremiah waited about twenty feet away, looking gleeful to finally have a reason to attack Jacob. The deputies marched Jacob over to their boss and one of the deputies kicked the back of Jacob's knee, forcing him to the ground. He stifled a groan as his arm was wrenched at an unnatural angle, the muscle's movement pushing the bullet deeper inside.

"Jacob Payne," the man said, smiling. "You are under arrest. What a shame to have such a promising career cut short."

"You have no authority to arrest me," Jacob said. "You're no sheriff. You're not even named John Horne. You're a fraud." He spat blood again, this time on Jeremiah's feet.

The outlaw jumped back, but blood still speckled the bottom of his pant legs. When he stepped forward again, he launched a kick into Jacob's ribs.

"Ah, you see, though, I have the power," he said as Jacob groaned in pain. "I have the deputies. I have the weapon. I am the sheriff of San Adrian, and I am declaring you guilty of assaulting a deputy."

"Fine," Jacob said, seeing his chance. "Let's pretend you can arrest me. Take me to a judge, and we'll see who is in custody then."

"Oh, Mr. Payne, perhaps you misheard me. I said that *I* find you guilty of the charge. Now to just decide on your sentence."

"Wait—" Timothy started.

"You're not the law," Jacob said, cutting the

boy off. "You need a judge. You don't get to decide guilt."

"No, I think you're guilty," Jeremiah said. "In fact, I'm sure of it. There's no need to bother taking you all the way to a judge in Tucson."

"You are not the law," Jacob said again, raising his voice for all to hear.

"I am now. I am the law, and I sentence you to death."

"What? No!" Timothy yelled.

Jacob struggled against his captors, but his injured arm put him at a disadvantage. He couldn't overpower three deputies with only one good arm, even if he was on his feet.

"Let go of me!" he cried. "You can't think this is right."

Deputy Nelson looked uncomfortable, but he didn't abandon his post. The other deputies held him fast. Jacob caught Maggie's eye across the crowd; her anguished expression made him wish he could shield her from this.

"No man is judge, jury, and executioner," Jacob shouted to the crowd.

He heard murmurs of confusion and protest all around, but it didn't seem as though any of them would be brave enough to stop the man. Jeremiah crossed the final steps to where Jacob was held kneeling on the ground.

Jacob took a deep breath and closed his eyes. He had done all he could to expose this alleged sheriff as the murderer he was. Just as Jacob felt the cold iron against his forehead, he heard the sound of several horses galloping up the street.

CHAPTER ELEVEN

With a gun pointed at his head, Jacob didn't dare turn to look to see who rode up the street, but he counted the hooves of three horses. The crowd that had gathered to watch the altercation began whispering and murmuring in confusion.

"Drop your weapon," Jacob heard a familiar voice say. "Step away from that man."

Instead of stepping away from him, Jeremiah grabbed Jacob's injured arm and yanked him to his feet. This was the first time the two men were so close together, and Jacob realized the outlaw only came up to his broad shoulders. The barrel of the gun was soon jammed hard into his ribs, still bruised from Blanchard's kick.

Jacob could feel the bruising deepen, but he stayed quiet, watching the riders arrive.

At the end of the street from the south side of town, and coming closer with every second, was Sheriff Williams of Bennettsville and two of his deputies.

"I said drop your weapon!" Sheriff Williams yelled. "Give up, Blanchard. Your reign is over."

Without dismounting, Sheriff Williams held up the wanted poster Jacob had last seen the morning before. Even from this distance, it was easy to identify Jeremiah Blanchard's scowling face.

"What are you doing here?" Jeremiah said to the sheriff of Bennettsville with a threatening growl.

"Upholding the law. One of these fine citizens of San Adrian telegraphed me to come identify you. You're not fooling anyone. Now come quietly so no one else gets hurt."

"The hell I will," Jeremiah said. "My deputies will arrest you for attempting to assault an officer of the law. Who says I'm the man in that poster?"

"*I* say," Jacob retorted. He was rewarded with a punch to the gut from Deputy Barnes.

"*I* say," Sheriff Williams echoed from on top of his horse.

"*I* say," Timothy said defiantly, making sure to stay close to Sheriff Williams and out of reach of any of the other San Adrian deputies. He raised his gun and pointed it at Jeremiah.

"You better watch yourself, kid," Jeremiah said.

Deputies Nelson and Conroy looked less and less sure, as the crowd around them grew more hostile, calling for this fight to end.

"Here. See for yourself." Sheriff Williams thrust the paper at the man nearest him, Deputy Conroy.

The deputy quickly scanned over the document. He shook his head. "The description matches. That's definitely him, even with this beard trying to cover his scar."

"You trying to hide your identity with that new scruff, Blanchard?" Jacob demanded. He felt the gun barrel dig deeper into his ribs.

"You murdered your wife?" Deputy Conroy said. "That's—" He shook his head, speechless.

Jeremiah removed his gun from Jacob's side and pointed it now at Deputy Conroy. "You got something to say? Huh? You want to try to take me on now that you know what I'm capable of?"

In the commotion, Jacob backed away, out of arm's reach from Jeremiah, and unfastened his hammer loop. He thought quickly. He could easily outdraw Jeremiah, but any bullets shot with this many people around ran the risk of injuring more than just their target. He didn't want to get shot, but more than that, he didn't trust the other man's aim.

Deputy Conroy thrust the wanted poster at Deputy Nelson. "Here. Read it."

Nelson scanned it quickly, spitting when he reached the end. "Woman killer," he hurled at Jeremiah.

"Murderer!" called a voice from the crowd.

Jeremiah turned from deputy to deputy, waving his gun around wildly. "I am the sheriff of this town!" he shouted. "You all need to *respect* me!" He fired his gun into the air.

That decided it for Jacob. He quickly drew his revolver, pulled the hammer back, aimed, and squeezed the trigger, landing his shot exactly in Jeremiah's right calf.

"Argh!" the outlaw cried, collapsing.

He was injured enough to keep him from running, as Jacob intended—but not enough to keep him from shooting. His aim was too wild to try to disarm him just yet.

"I am the sheriff!" he shouted again, though it was somewhat distorted by his moan of pain.

"Not any more," Jacob said. "There is no Sheriff Horne. There never was."

"You thought you'd get away with changing your name just because you had destroyed the wanted bill?" Timothy said. He was still holding his jaw from where Jacob had punched him, but his anger shone through in spite of whatever pain he might still be in.

"You destroyed the wanted poster, too?" Deputy Conroy said, marveling. "That is low. That's not upholding the law. Where is your respect for your duty?" He took a deep breath and deliberately turned his gun to point at Jeremiah.

The outlaw cursed, but still would not surrender. He fired again toward Sheriff Williams, but it went high and wide.

"Sheriff Williams," Jacob said, offering his last nail in the coffin. "When you take this man before the judge, be sure you let him know Blanchard is under suspicion for murdering at least one more man. Sheriff Winthrop died while alone in the desert with Blanchard. I don't think that's a coincidence. Mr. Charles, the undertaker of this town, has agreed to testify about what he witnessed when the body came in."

"Sheriff Winthrop, too?" Deputy Nelson shook his head, relaxing his gun arm and looking dejected for just a short moment. He stopped himself, looking up again and glaring at Jeremiah. He took a deep breath and in one quick step moved from pointing his gun at Jacob, to pointing it at Jeremiah, now joining his fellow deputies.

The outlaw let out a frustrated hiss. "You'll regret that."

"You get one last chance, Blanchard. Surrender. You no longer have even a single deputy on your side," Jacob said.

Jeremiah growled, glaring at Jacob. He looked around, realizing how many guns were pointed at him. Even Ed Baker had a Winchester in his arms, trained at the man. The tide had turned. Deputy Barnes had left his side, and was now standing closer to Jacob, with his gun holstered, arms harmlessly at his side.

Seeing his last ally had deserted him, Jeremiah cursed, tossed his gun to the ground, and surrendered.

CHAPTER TWELVE

While many guns were still pointed at the outlaw, the Bennettsville deputies dismounted and bound him, wrists and ankles together. As soon as it was clear that Jeremiah Blanchard had been contained, Jacob finally let himself relax. He had done his job; the town was safe again.

The moment he felt himself let his guard down, Jacob spotted Maggie Winthrop's gleaming hair pushing through the crowd. Her expression was frantic as she checked on Timothy. Once she had ascertained that he was fine, she turned to Jacob.

"Let me clean you up," Maggie said. She took his uninjured arm and led Jacob to the boardwalk on the side of the street, guiding him to sit down. The sleeve was torn and bloody where the bullet had gone in. "I'm going to have to tear your shirt, Mr. Payne."

"That's all right. With the reward from catching Blanchard I can get a new shirt," he said with a smile.

She handed him a small bottle of whiskey. He took only a mouthful while she washed and disinfected his wound.

"This is going to hurt," she said softly.

He nodded. "Go ahead." He had been shot before. He'd had bullets extracted before. He knew what to expect, but that wouldn't make it hurt any less. He balled up his fist as she carefully, delicately pulled the bullet out of his bicep with a pair of tongs. He didn't move, he didn't squirm, he didn't cry out, and she was done in no time.

"Now, you really should rest a bit," Maggie said, fixing his bandage over the wound. "I don't want to hear about you getting in any fights or inspiring any shootouts for at least a couple hours."

Jacob laughed. "A couple hours? No promises, but I think I can handle that."

"If you come to supper at our home tonight, that should keep you busy for at least a little while. You won't be able to peel potatoes, though."

"Then I guess we won't be eating potatoes," he said with a laugh.

She smiled but then grew serious, bending her face closer to his. "Jacob," she began in a quiet voice. "That is, Mr. Payne. I need to thank you for what you did for us. For me. I never thought I would see justice for my Alex, and then you come to town and not only uncover the truth of his death but also rid our town of his murderer."

"It's my job, ma'am. I'm happy to do it." He wanted to put his arm around her, to squeeze her hand, to comfort her in some way, but he knew he had done all he could. "I'm just glad you weren't around to see the part of my job where I had to rough up your nephew."

She smiled. "I stayed away from that as much as I could. Knowing it had to happen was one thing. Seeing it happen would have been quite another. Although, that reminds me . . . maybe I'll set you to cleaning bloodstains out of Timothy's shirt when you come over later."

Jacob grinned. "Whatever I can do to pull my weight."

"Oh, Mr. Payne!" Mrs. Finch exclaimed as she burst through the crowd. "Mr. Payne, that was so brave of you. I knew, *we* knew, there was something not right about Sheriff Horne, but I never would have dreamed he was such a horrible character."

A round man, shorter than her, stood just behind Mrs. Finch, his hands stuffed in his pockets as he let her lead the way.

Jacob stood to greet them, keeping his left arm resting at his side. "This must be Mr. Finch."

"Norman Finch, at your service. We've upgraded your room at the Wildflower Hotel. We're hoping you'll still stay the night with us before moving on again."

"You didn't have to do that."

"Oh, Mr. Payne, you must stay," Mrs. Finch gushed. "And come to supper at our home. Give me your laundry to do before you leave. There must be something more we can do for you."

"That's very kind of you, ma'am. I've already made plans for supper, but I'm much obliged for the room."

"Mr. Payne, can I speak to you?" Sheriff Williams said, interrupting the women's fawning.

The sheriff led the way to the San Adrian jail and let himself in.

Jacob again found himself watching out the window of a jail while the sheriff escorted one of his captures. This time, though, instead of taking the thief to a cell in this jail, Jacob watched the Bennettsville deputy ride off to their own jail with Jeremiah Blanchard in tow. He was lashed to a horse, and none too gently.

When he returned from giving his deputy instructions, Sheriff Williams lowered his giant frame into the chair behind the desk of the San Adrian jail. "Can't say this fits me any better than the chair at home." He dug through the mess of paperwork on the desk to find a pencil and scrap of paper to make a note. "Well, Payne, that's a second reward for you in just as many days. Since we don't have the cash on hand, where do you want this one sent?"

"Wire it to Mrs. Maggie Winthrop in San Adrian."

"All of it, Payne? What are you hunting bounties for if you're just going to give all the money to someone else?"

"This man murdered her husband, and she was just as useful in getting him caught as I was. She deserves the reward and she can use the help. This will keep her from having to worry about money for a while."

"Want me to send a telegram along with it?"

"No. She doesn't need to know who it's from."

"She'll know."

Jacob smiled. "She might guess, but I'll never say—and you'd better not either."

"You're a good man, Payne. As long as you swear to me you won't go hungry by giving up this money, I'm happy to pass it along to the sheriff's widow."

"Thanks, Sheriff."

"You know where you're off to next? San Adrian might like to see you stand for Sheriff now that Horne—I mean Jeremiah—is gone."

"No. Thank you. I'm not meant to be stuck in one spot very long. There will be another criminal that crosses my path sooner if I move on to the next town. I'll stay here another night, enjoy another supper with Mrs. Winthrop and give the Finches my business, but I'll be on my way in the morning. Thank you all the same."

"Well, in that case, how about that drink I promised you before you head to supper?" Sheriff Williams asked.

"I'll take you up on that. I bet Ed would be happy to see us," Jacob responded with a smile.

ALSO BY A.T. BUTLER

DOWNLOAD MY FREE SHORT STORY at

ATBUTLER.COM/FREE

———

Jacob Payne Series:

Trouble By Any Name

Danger in the Canyon

Justice for Jasper

Blood on the Mountain
Outlaw Country

Jacob Payne, bounty hunter, is on the heels of another dangerous outlaw.

Tracking a bank robber through the Arizona desert, Jacob has to contend with snakes, falling rocks, and other dangers like running out of water. Will his back east survival skills keep him safe from everything the desert--and the outlaw--has to throw at him?

Grab your copy on Amazon today!

Jacob Payne dismounted. The relentless, scorching Arizona sun beat down, drenching his dark, close-cropped hair with sweat and plastering it to his skull. With one hand he took off his hat to fan his face, and with the other took hold of the reins to lead his pinto down through the uneven, rocky bank of the dry river bed. The sandy ground shifted and crumbled under his feet. As he took the first step through the brush, the dirt bank collapsed and one of the ragweed plants uprooted altogether. Jacob almost lost his balance as he slipped down the low slope. Going so long without water, even a desert plant couldn't hang on forever, and Jacob knew he would be the same way. A body could only take so much.

The tall man paused to let the dirt and rocks tumble down the rest of the bank while he replaced his hat. His shirt clung to his sides, tight across his broad shoulders, the sweat running down his back under the layers. He blinked back the sweat dripping into his eyes. Once the rocks had settled he would lead his horse across, searching again for both water and his man. He couldn't risk his horse making a false step. He couldn't risk sweating out all his water. He still had a ways to go.

The bounty hunter had been on the outlaw's trail for three days from Tucson, winding far to the south and the west following his mark. While he thought he had packed enough water when he set out, the canteen was running low now. He had been able to supplement a little along the way, but if he didn't find a substantial source of water soon he might have to give up this hunt.

Jacob had never walked away from a reward once he started tracking and he had no intention of starting now. The man he was after would need water just as badly, and Jacob knew he could best him.

ABOUT THE AUTHOR

I grew up in the southwest—California Missions, snakes and constant threat of drought weaving the backdrop of my childhood.

But it wasn't until I moved to Texas a few years ago that the magic and mythology of the American West began to seep into my soul.

I'd love to write about Jacob Payne for a long time. ...

If you enjoyed this book, a review on your favorite retailer would be greatly appreciated.

- A

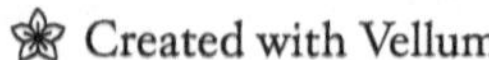 Created with Vellum

www.ingramcontent.com/pod-product-compliance
Lightning Source LLC
Chambersburg PA
CBHW032040180726
48284CB00008B/2686